EDGE BOOKS™

Forensic Crime Solvers

Insect Evidence

by Michael Martin

Consultant:
Robert D. Hall, PhD, JD
Associate Vice Chancellor for Research and Director of Compliance
Office of Research
University of Missouri, Columbia

Capstone press®

Mankato, Minnesota

Edge Books are published by Capstone Press,
151 Good Counsel Drive, P.O. Box 669, Mankato, Minnesota 56002.
www.capstonepress.com

Library of Congress Cataloging-in-Publication Data
Martin, Michael, 1948–
    Insect evidence / by Michael Martin.
    p. cm.—(Edge books. Forensic crime solvers)
    Includes bibliographical references and index.
    ISBN-13: 978-0-7368-6789-4 (hardcover)
    ISBN-10: 0-7368-6789-9 (hardcover)
    ISBN-13: 978-0-7368-7873-9 (softcover pbk.)
    ISBN-10: 0-7368-7873-4 (softcover pbk.)
    1. Forensic entomology—Juvenile literature. I. Title. II. Series.
RA1063.45.M37 2007
614'.1—dc22   2006024889

Summary: Discusses how forensic entomologists use insect evidence to solve crimes.

Editorial Credits
Angie Kaelberer, editor; Juliette Peters, set designer; Ted Williams, book designer;
    Wanda Winch, photo researcher/photo editor

Photo Credits
Capstone Press/Karon Dubke, 4, 6, 7, 8, 27
Corbis/Otto Rogge, 24
Creatas, 26
Digital Vision, 19
Getty Images Inc./Darren McCollester, front cover, 28; Jeff Topping, 29
Penn State University/Dept. of Entomology/Krista Kahler, 17
Photo courtesy of Dr. William M. Bass, Forensic Anthropologist, 20
Photo Researchers Inc./John Mitchell, 13; Pascal Goetgheluck, 18; Stephen Dalton, 12
Shutterstock/Thomas Mounsey, 21; Tim Zurowski, back cover
Unicorn Stock Photos/Jim Shippee, 10
University of Florida/IFAS Communication Services/Thomas Wright, 15, 22
Visuals Unlimited/Dr. James L. Castner, 1, 14

1 2 3 4 5 6 12 11 10 09 08 07

Table of Contents

CHAPTER 1

Maggots and Murder

One spring day, Nathan Russell and his friend Randy Peterson walked home from school. The boys took a shortcut through a wooded area. Suddenly, they noticed a bad smell. The odor led the boys to an area of tall grass.

Something lay on the ground, half-hidden by the grass. At first, the boys thought it was a dead animal. Then they saw jeans and a pair of shoes. Neither boy wanted to get any closer. They ran to the nearest house and called the police.

The Crime Scene

A few minutes later, a police officer arrived. The boys led him into the woods. There, the officer found the dead body of a young woman.

◀ Nathan and Randy couldn't believe what they stumbled upon.

The body was covered with fly eggs that had hatched into larvae called maggots. The hungry maggots crawled over the woman's body.

The officer called in a medical examiner (ME) and a crime scene investigator (CSI). Meanwhile, other police officers arrived. They placed tape around the crime scene so it could be studied for clues.

The cause of death became clear when the ME looked for injuries to the body. A blow to the back of the head had crushed the woman's skull.

A CSI helped the police officer collect evidence from the scene.

The CSI carefully placed maggots in a specimen jar.

Bugs with Stories

The ME and the CSI knew that a woman had been reported missing the day before. The body and its clothing matched the missing woman's description.

The CSI plucked the maggots from the corpse with tweezers. He kept some of the maggots alive. He put the other maggots in jars of alcohol to preserve them.

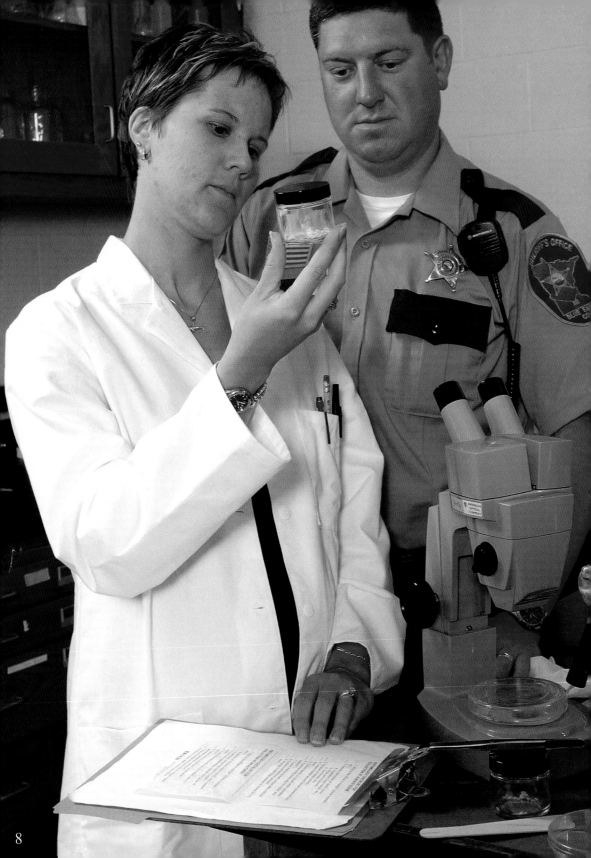

The CSI brought the bugs to a forensic entomologist. Entomologists study insects. Forensic entomologists use their knowledge of insects to help solve crimes.

Tracking a Killer

Entomologist Lisa Johnson knew what kind of blow fly laid the eggs that became the maggots. In warm weather, these maggots take 16 to 24 hours to reach the size of those on the body. That information helped Johnson determine the woman's time of death. Johnson told police the eggs were laid the day before. That meant the victim was dead at that time.

Two days earlier, witnesses had seen a man with the victim. The police suspected he was the killer. When they searched his apartment, they found bloodstains. DNA tests proved it was the victim's blood. Soon after, the man confessed to the murder.

◀ The size of the maggots helped Johnson determine the woman's time of death.

CHAPTER 2

CRIME SCENE DO NOT CROSS CRIME SCENE DO NOT CROSS CRIME SCENE DO NOT CROSS CRIME SCENE DO NOT CROSS CRIME SCENE DO NOT CROSS

Learn about:

- Blow flies
- Maggot life cycle
- Later predators

Insect Invasion

Nature uses insects to clean up dead bodies. Luckily for forensic entomologists, these clean-up artists tend to arrive in a set order.

When an animal or human dies outdoors, the first insects to show up are usually blow flies. Blow flies have an unusually keen sense of smell. Female blow flies can smell blood and rotting flesh from at least 1 mile (1.6 kilometers) away.

Clues That Crawl

About 90 kinds of blow flies live in the United States. Each type has a slightly different life cycle, but most blow flies are active only during warm weather.

Forensic entomologists use the blow fly's life cycle to find out when a death occurred. This is possible because the bug's development follows a set pattern.

◄ Insects are often the first visitors to a crime scene.

A few hours after a death, a female blow fly lands on the corpse and lays between 200 and 500 eggs. In warm weather, the eggs hatch within 16 to 24 hours. The newly hatched maggots feed on the corpse for seven to 12 days, depending on the type of fly. The maggots then crawl away to a dry place and become pupae. During this stage, the maggot's outer body hardens into a case. Inside, the maggot changes into a fly. About 18 to 24 days later, the adult blow fly comes out of the case.

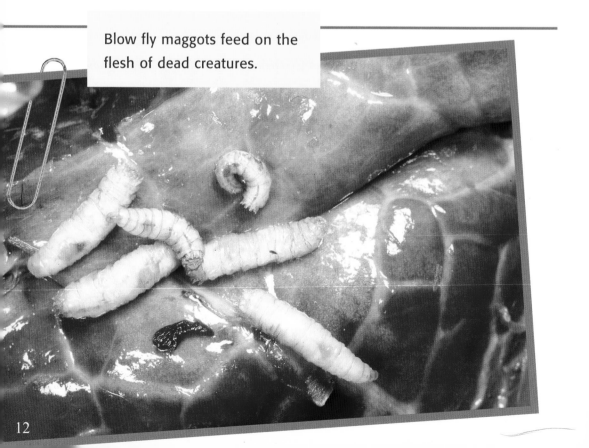

Blow fly maggots feed on the flesh of dead creatures.

Flesh flies follow blow flies in nature's clean-up chain.

Other Insect Helpers

Blow flies are the first insects to visit a dead body. But they are not the only bugs to help investigators. As a body decays, several kinds of bugs arrive at different times. Flesh flies appear about four days after the person dies. By that time, gases have built up in the body. The flesh flies lay their eggs on the bloated corpse. The larvae are born live and immediately begin feeding on the flesh.

Carrion beetles feed on other insects, as well as flesh.

A day or two later, wasps and beetles show up to eat the fly eggs and larvae. Some of them also feed on the fluids that drain out of the collapsing corpse.

Most of the body's flesh is gone three to eight weeks after death. By then, mites and moths are feeding on the body's dried skin and hair.

Collecting Evidence

Any insect found on or near a corpse can be evidence. CSIs and entomologists collect insects and pupa cases. Most of the insects are preserved in alcohol. But many bugs look alike during their earliest stages of life. Even entomologists can't always tell them apart. That is why some eggs or larvae are kept alive. Once the bugs become adults, the entomologist can tell police exactly what kind of bugs they are dealing with.

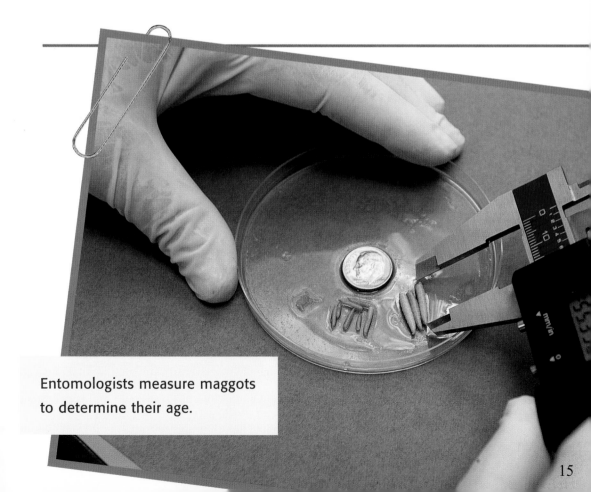

Entomologists measure maggots to determine their age.

CHAPTER 3

Learn about:

- Insects in the lab
- Time of death
- The Body Farm

The Bug Experts

Identifying the type of bugs found on or near a body is just the first step. After that, the forensic entomologist starts determining the time of death. They do so by working backward.

Suppose a certain kind of blow fly maggots are found on a dead body. An entomologist measures the maggots' size and discovers that they are two hours old. He knows this type of fly's eggs hatch in about 12 hours. He also knows that blow flies don't lay eggs at night. The entomologist determines that the victim died the day before.

◀ A forensic entomologist's work often starts at the crime scene.

Warm, sunny weather can affect how insects behave.

Much to Learn

Thousands of bugs feed on decaying flesh. Forensic entomologists must be familiar with the life cycles of all these types of bugs. Entomologists also consider the weather and the time of year.

Insects act differently on sunny, warm days than they do on cloudy, rainy ones. Some insects are more active during certain seasons. Also, illegal drugs like cocaine and heroin can speed up maggots' development. If a dead person has these drugs in his or her system, the maggots may be younger than others of their size.

Entomologists sometimes study dead animals to learn more about how insects feed on a corpse. They often use dead pigs. Pigs attract the same kinds of bugs that dead people do.

Scientists often use pigs in forensic entomology.

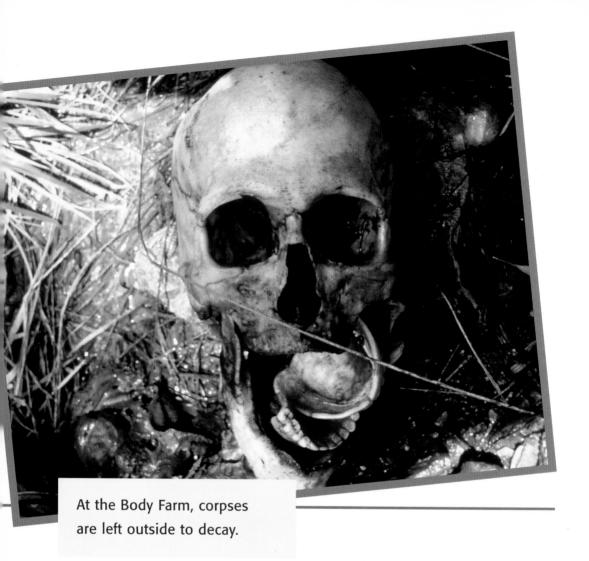

At the Body Farm, corpses are left outside to decay.

Studying Decay

Sometimes forensic entomologists study how human bodies decompose. They can do that at the Forensic Anthropology Center at the University of Tennessee in Knoxville. The center is better known as the Body Farm. Corpses are left outdoors in a small, fenced-in area.

Most of the corpses are people who donated their bodies to science. Some are buried. Some are left out in the open. Others are placed in the trunks of cars.

Whether a body is lying in shade, in sun, or inside a car or house affects how fast it decomposes. Even the type of clothing on the body can affect decay.

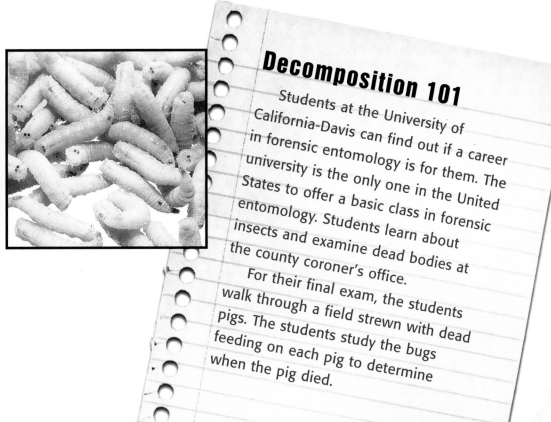

Decomposition 101

Students at the University of California-Davis can find out if a career in forensic entomology is for them. The university is the only one in the United States to offer a basic class in forensic entomology. Students learn about insects and examine dead bodies at the county coroner's office.

For their final exam, the students walk through a field strewn with dead pigs. The students study the bugs feeding on each pig to determine when the pig died.

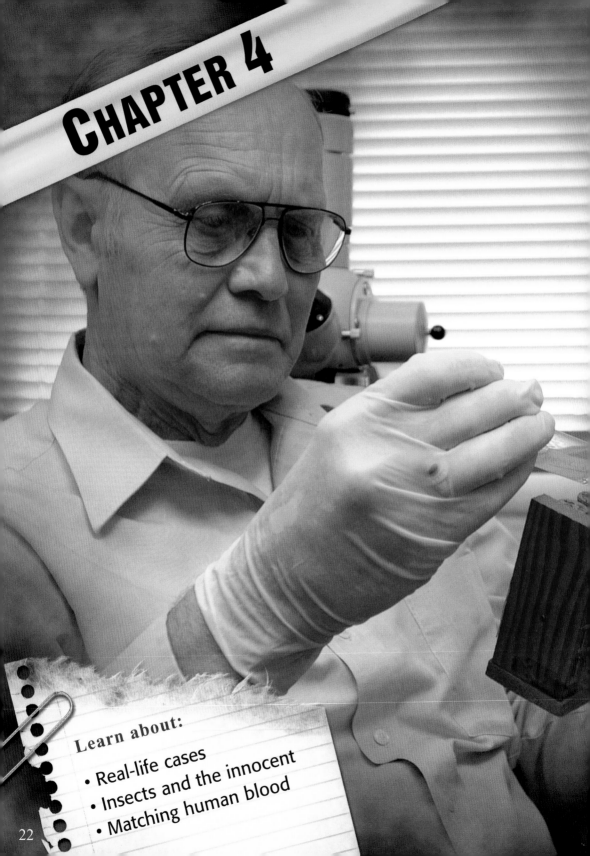

CHAPTER 4

Learn about:
- Real-life cases
- Insects and the innocent
- Matching human blood

Ask the Insects

Insect evidence has helped solve many horrible crimes. One happened in San Diego, California, in 1984. College student Anne Swanke vanished while walking toward her car. Four days later, a hiker found Swanke's body. Her throat had been slashed.

Police suspected the killer was a man named David Lucas. But Lucas could prove he was somewhere else on three of the days Swanke was missing. Then a forensic entomologist examined the tiny blow fly eggs found on Swanke's body. He found they were from a kind of blow fly that lays eggs only when the temperature is above 68 degrees Fahrenheit (20 degrees Celsius).

◀ Insect evidence has helped solve a number of crimes.

Many flies need warm
weather to hatch.

A check of weather records showed that the only day the temperature got above 68 degrees was the day the woman disappeared. That was also the only day for which Lucas couldn't account for where he was. A jury convicted him of murder.

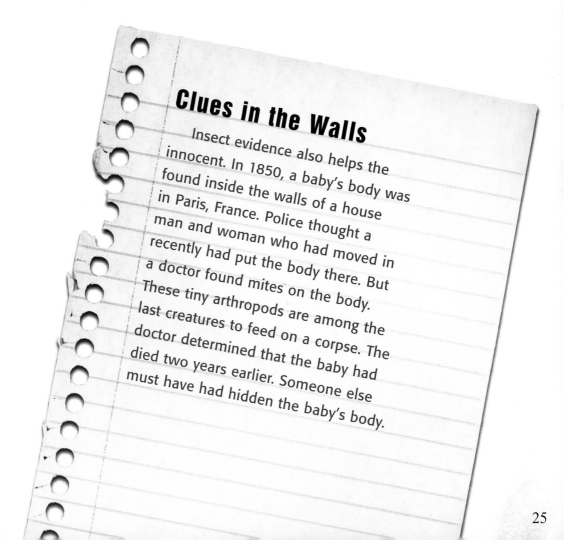

Clues in the Walls

Insect evidence also helps the innocent. In 1850, a baby's body was found inside the walls of a house in Paris, France. Police thought a man and woman who had moved in recently had put the body there. But a doctor found mites on the body. These tiny arthropods are among the last creatures to feed on a corpse. The doctor determined that the baby had died two years earlier. Someone else must have had hidden the baby's body.

Piles of garbage at landfills can hide bodies.

More Clues That Catch Killers

Bugs also provide clues about what happens
after a murder. In 1995, a woman's body was found
at a landfill in Maryland. Eggs from a fly that
lays eggs only in shady places were on the body.

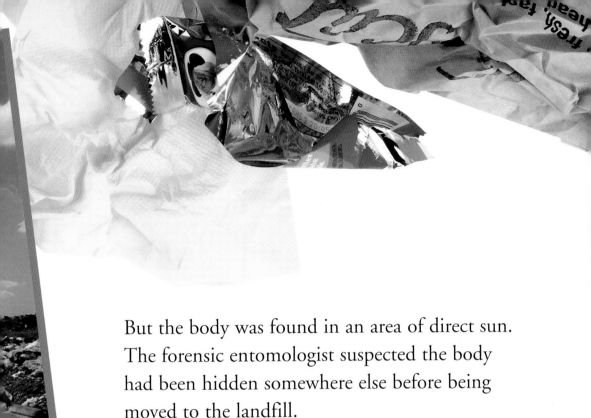

But the body was found in an area of direct sun. The forensic entomologist suspected the body had been hidden somewhere else before being moved to the landfill.

This information helped police arrest the killer. He was a truck driver who had kept the body in his trailer for several days.

Even the lack of insects can solve a crime. In one case, a man told police he had found his girlfriend murdered in her home. All the windows in the house were open. The man said he thought that was how the killer got in. But an autopsy showed the woman had been dead for 12 hours. Since there were no flies on her body, the windows must have been opened just before the police came. The man was found guilty of murder.

Entomologists examine mosquitoes for clues.

Blood-sucking Bugs

CSIs sometimes collect blood-sucking mosquitoes and mites at crime scenes. If the type of blood inside these arthropods does or doesn't match that of the victim, it can be an important clue.

In some cases, scientists can identify DNA from human blood found inside an insect. This information tells CSIs whose blood it is. If the CSIs are really lucky, they might even match the blood with that of a killer.

Forensic entomologists are always discovering new ways for insects to help them solve crimes. It seems certain that their tiny helpers will send more criminals to prison in the future.

Scientists can obtain DNA from human blood inside mosquitoes.

Glossary

arthropod (AR-thruh-pod)—an animal with a hard outer shell and many legs with joints

autopsy (AW-top-see)—an examination performed on a dead body to find the cause of death

corpse (KORPS)—a dead body

decompose (dee-kuhm-POZE)—to rot or decay

DNA (dee-en-AYE)—material in cells that gives people their individual characteristics; DNA stands for deoxyribonucleic acid.

entomologist (en-tuh-MAH-luh-jist)—a scientist who studies insects

larva (LAR-vuh)—an insect at the stage of development between an egg and a pupa when it looks like a worm; more than one larva are larvae.

maggot (MAG-uht)—the larva of certain flies

pupa (PYOO-puh)—an insect at the stage of development between a larva and an adult; more than one pupa are pupae.

Read More

Platt, Richard. *Forensics*. Kingfisher Knowledge. Boston: Kingfisher, 2005.

Rollins, Barbara B., and Michael Dahl. *Cause of Death*. Forensic Crime Solvers. Mankato, Minn.: Capstone Press, 2004.

Walker, Maryalice. *Entomology and Palynology: Evidence from the Natural World*. Forensics, the Science of Crime-Solving. Philadelphia: Mason Crest, 2006.

Internet Sites

FactHound offers a safe, fun way to find Internet sites related to this book. All of the sites on FactHound have been researched by our staff.

Here's how:

1. Visit *www.facthound.com*

2. Choose your grade level.

3. Type in this book ID **0736867899** for age-appropriate sites. You may also browse subjects by clicking on letters, or by clicking on pictures and words.

4. Click on the **Fetch It** button.

FactHound will fetch the best sites for you!

Index